PURCHASED WI

TITLE II - F

D0385713

A Goat for Carlo

By Judith Lawrence

Drawings by Liz Dauber

GARRARD PUBLISHING COMPANY
CHAMPAIGN, ILLINOIS

St. Benedict School
300 N. 7th St.
Cambridge, Ohio 43725

Copyright © 1971 by Thomas Nelson & Sons (Canada), Limited All rights reserved. Manufactured in the U.S.A.
Standard Book Number: 8116–6709–X Library of Congress Catalog Card Number: 79–161028

A Goat for Carlo

This was the day
Carlo had waited for.
He and his father
were going to buy a goat.
Carlo ate breakfast quickly.
"Our goat will be beautiful,"
he said to his mother.

"She'll have little black feet
and big brown eyes.
Her coat will be soft and shiny."
"Hurry, Carlo,"
said his mother.
Carlo's father was waiting.
"There will be many goats
in the market today," he said.

"We'll pick out
the one we want."
They walked down the hill
toward the town.
On the way, they met
many of their friends.

"We're going to buy a goat,"
Carlo called to them,
"a most beautiful goat."
"I hope you find
the one you want,"
shouted one friend.
"We will, we will," called Carlo.

The market was a busy place.

"Goats, goats, goats,"

shouted an old man.

"Do you want

to buy a goat?"

the man asked Carlo.

"Yes," said Carlo.

"Show us your best goat."
The man showed them
a beautiful goat.
Her hair was soft and shiny.
She had little black feet
and big brown eyes.

"Father," said Carlo,
"this is the goat we want.
She's the most beautiful goat
I've ever seen."
"How much is she?"
Carlo asked the man.

When the man told them,
Carlo's father was sad.
"We don't have enough money."
Carlo and his father
started to walk away.
"Wait! Wait!" called the man.
"How much money
do you have?"
Carlo's father showed his money
to the old man.
"I have another goat
I didn't show you,"
said the old man.
"No one wants her
for she is small and thin.

You can have her
for very little money."
"Please," said Carlo,
"show us the goat."
The old man
showed them the goat.
She came to Carlo.

St. Benedict Elem. Sch. Lib 1

She looked at him
and sniffed his hand.
"What a sad face!" said Carlo.
"She's not beautiful,
but I think she likes me."
"We'll buy her,"
said Carlo's father.

"Come, little goat,"
said Carlo.
"You'll have a good home."
Carlo's friend, Pedro,
called to him,
"Where did you get
that funny goat, Carlo?"

"She's not funny," said Carlo.
"She's beautiful!"
"What are you going
to call her?"
asked another friend.
"I'm going to call her Tina,"
said Carlo.

Tina trotted up the path
behind Carlo and his father.
"Look, Father," said Carlo.
"Tina doesn't look sad now.
I think she knows
we'll be good to her."

That night, Carlo made a cart
for Tina.
"She'll help us with our work,"
he said to his father.
"Tomorrow we'll have
eight bags of onions
to sell in the market.
Tina can pull them
on the cart.
You won't have to go
to the market."

The next morning,
Carlo put the bags
of onions
in the cart.
Tina pulled, and the cart
began to move.
"Good-bye," called Carlo.

The goat trotted
down the path.
The little cart
bumped along behind her.
When they reached the market,
Carlo found a place
to put the cart.

Tina waited nearby.
Carlo began to call out,
"I have onions to sell!"
A woman stopped
and looked at the onions.
"Did you grow these?"
she asked.

"Yes," said Carlo.
The woman bought some.
Carlo put the money
in his little bag.
Many other people
bought his vegetable.
At noon Carlo stopped
to eat his lunch.
Suddenly he heard something.
Crunch! Crunch! Crunch!
The boy looked behind him.
Tina was eating his straw hat.
"Oh, Tina!" he said.
"You're hungry."

Carlo bought some carrots
for Tina's lunch.
Soon all the onions
were sold.
"It's time to go home,"
Carlo told Tina.

Tina trotted up the path,
pulling the little cart.
As they climbed higher,
Carlo saw some pretty flowers.
"Wait, Tina," he said.
"I'll pick some for Mother."

At the top of the path
Carlo met his father.
"I sold all the onions,"
he said.
"Good," said his father.
"You and Tina
have done well."
Carlo gave the flowers
to his mother.
She thanked him.
"What happened
to your hat?"
she asked.
"Where is it?"

"Tina was so hungry
she ate it
when I wasn't looking,"
Carlo answered.
His mother laughed.
"I'll make you another hat.
We have enough straw," she said.

When they had finished eating,
Carlo fed Tina.
She was very hungry.
"You're a good goat, Tina,"
said Carlo.
"I'm glad you came
to live with us."

"Maaa," answered Tina.
"Good night, little goat,"
said Carlo.

One evening
Carlo couldn't find Tina.
He looked in the fields
near his home.
He walked up and down
calling her name.
Tina did not come.

"I'm afraid she's lost,"
said Carlo.
"She'll come back,"
said Carlo's father.
"She can't be faraway."
"By now Tina has found
a safe place to sleep,"
said Carlo's mother.
In the morning
Carlo looked for Tina,
but he couldn't find her.
"Maybe she has gone
down the hill to the market,"
said Carlo's father.

"You should look there."
"I will," said Carlo.
He hurried down the hill.
He asked some people
if they'd seen his goat.
No one had seen her.
Sadly Carlo went home.

That night, after Carlo
had gone to bed,
he thought he heard Tina.
"Maaa, maaa."
He got up quickly
and went outside.

Again he thought
he heard Tina calling,
"Maaa, maaa."
"It *is* Tina!"
he said to himself.
He awakened his father.
"I heard Tina calling,"
Carlo told him.
"She must be
high up on the mountain."
"I'll get the lantern,"
said his father.
Carlo and his father climbed
the mountain path.

It was cold
on the mountain.
The sky was black,
and there was no moon.
The light from the lantern
helped them to see.

Carlo kept calling,
"Tina! Tina!
Where are you?"
Finally they heard her,
"Maaa, maaa."
Suddenly Carlo stopped.

There in the long grass
he saw Tina.
By the light of the lantern
he saw a baby goat beside her.
"Look, Father!" said Carlo softly.
"Tina has a beautiful baby.

It has soft, shiny hair
and little black feet."
Carlo's father
picked up the baby.

Carlo took the lantern.
Tina trotted behind them.
Carlo's mother was waiting
for them at the house.
"How beautiful the baby is!"
she said.

She got some straw.
She made a bed
for Tina and her baby.
Carlo spoke softly to Tina,
"Now you're safe, Tina,
and your baby is too!"
"Maaa," said Tina.

One day Carlo's father said,
"It's time for you and Tina
to go to the market.
We have many bags
of onions to sell."
Carlo put the bags
in the cart.
He and Tina
started down the path.
The little goat
trotted behind them.
They hadn't gone far
when Pedro called,
"Carlo!

Where did you get
that beautiful little goat?"
"It's Tina's baby,"
answered Carlo.
"Now we have
two fine goats to love!"

1956

E
LAW
LAWRENCE, JUDITH
A goat for Carlo

DATE DUE			
SEP 2 3 1975			
OCT 1 5 1975			
OCT 2 9 1975			
MAR 9 1976			
OCT 3 1977			
OCT 1 7 1977			
NOV 1 1977			
SEP 2 4 78			

DEMCO